Full STEAM Ahead!
Technology Time

Parts Work Together

Cynthia O'Brien

CRABTREE
PUBLISHING COMPANY
WWW.CRABTREEBOOKS.COM

Title-Specific Learning Objectives:
Readers will:
- Understand that technologies are made of parts that work together.
- Explain how the parts of a bicycle work together in a system.
- Identify key ideas in the text and explain them in their own words.

High-frequency words (grade one)	Academic vocabulary
a, and, are, go, help, is, make, of, the, you	chain, connect, frame, lens, pedal, system, technology

Before, During, and After Reading Prompts:

Activate Prior Knowledge and Make Predictions:
Have children read the title and look at the cover images. Ask them:
- What do you think this book will be about?
- Look around the classroom. Can you find something with more than one part? How do its parts work together?

During Reading:
After reading pages 6 and 7, ask children to talk with an elbow partner about the main idea of the spread. Bring the discussion back to the full group. Ask children:

- What is the main idea on pages 6 and 7?
- What examples and pictures does the author use to help you understand the main idea?
- Can you think of any other examples?

After Reading:
Discuss why it is important that all parts of a technology work as they should. Examine the labeled diagram on pages 8 and 9. Invite children to choose another example from the book or from around the classroom. In groups, have them sketch a diagram of the technology and label its parts. Invite groups to present their diagrams. Talk about how the parts work together to let the technology work as it should.

Author: Cynthia O'Brien
Series Development: Reagan Miller
Editor: Janine Deschenes
Proofreader: Melissa Boyce
STEAM Notes for Educators: Janine Deschenes
Guided Reading Leveling: Publishing Solutions Group

Cover, Interior Design, and Prepress: Samara Parent
Photo research: Cynthia O'Brien and Samara Parent
Production coordinator: Katherine Berti
Photographs:
iStock: LeManna: front cover; Wavebreakmedia: p. 4; wundervisuals: p. 6; SeventyFour: p. 21 (top)
All other photographs by Shutterstock

Library and Archives Canada Cataloguing in Publication

O'Brien, Cynthia (Cynthia J.), author
    Parts work together / Cynthia O'Brien.

(Full STEAM ahead!)
Includes index.
Issued in print and electronic formats.
ISBN 978-0-7787-6201-0 (hardcover).--
ISBN 978-0-7787-6238-6 (softcover).--ISBN 978-1-4271-2257-5 (HTML)

    1. Technology--Juvenile literature. 2. Machinery--Juvenile literature. I. Title.

T48.O27 2019   j600   C2018-906159-6
                                                C2018-906160-X

Library of Congress Cataloging-in-Publication Data

Names: O'Brien, Cynthia (Cynthia J.), author.
Title: Parts work together / Cynthia O'Brien.
Description: New York, New York : Crabtree Publishing Company, [2019] | Series: Full steam ahead! | Includes index.
Identifiers: LCCN 2018056584 (print) | LCCN 2018056890 (ebook) | ISBN 9781427122575 (Electronic) | ISBN 9780778762010 (hardcover : alk. paper) | ISBN 9780778762386 (pbk. : alk. paper)
Subjects: LCSH: Machine parts--Juvenile literature.
Classification: LCC TJ243 (ebook) | LCC TJ243 .O27 2019 (print) | DDC 621.8/2--dc23
LC record available at https://lccn.loc.gov/2018056584

Printed in the U.S.A./042019/CG20190215

Table of Contents

Made of Parts............ 4
Working Together..... 6
Parts of a Bicycle...... 8
Make it Move 10
Push the Pedals....... 12
Something to Hold.................... 14
The Seat and Frame................ 16
Every Part is Important.................. 18
Working Well 20
Words to Know....... 22
Index and About the Author.... 23
Crabtree Plus Digital Code........... 23
STEAM Notes for Educators................ 24

Crabtree Publishing Company
www.crabtreebooks.com   1-800-387-7650

Copyright © **2019 CRABTREE PUBLISHING COMPANY.** All rights reserved. No part of this publication may be reproduced, stored in a retrieval system or be transmitted in any form or by any means, electronic, mechanical, photocopying, recording, or otherwise, without the prior written permission of Crabtree Publishing Company. In Canada: We acknowledge the financial support of the Government of Canada through the Book Publishing Industry Development Program (BPIDP) for our publishing activities.

Published in Canada
Crabtree Publishing
616 Welland Ave.
St. Catharines, Ontario
L2M 5V6

Published in the United States
Crabtree Publishing
PMB 59051
350 Fifth Avenue, 59th Floor
New York, New York 10118

Published in the United Kingdom
Crabtree Publishing
Maritime House
Basin Road North, Hove
BN41 1WR

Published in Australia
Crabtree Publishing
Unit 3 – 5 Currumbin Court
Capalaba
QLD 4157

Made of Parts

A technology is a tool that helps us do work. People create technologies to make life easier, safer, and more fun.

shelf · pencil · computer · chair

How many technologies can you see in this picture?

4

Many technologies are made of different parts.

A seesaw is made of parts. It has seats and handles for people to use. It has parts that help it move up and down.

5

Working Together

The parts of a technology work together to form a **system**. They make the technology do its job.

lenses

arm

Sunglasses **protect** your eyes from the Sun. They have parts that work together. **Lenses** block some of the Sun's **rays**. Arms hold the glasses in place.

button

lens

A camera has many parts. We look through a lens. We click a button to take a photo. All of the parts work together.

7

Parts of a Bicycle

A bicycle is a technology. It makes it easier and more fun to get from place to place.

seat

chain

A bicycle has a system of many parts. Together, they make the bicycle work.

Do you know these bicycle parts?

8

handlebars

brakes

frame

pedal

wheels

9

Make it Move

A bicycle has two wheels. The wheels turn. They make the bicycle move forward.

wheels

A bicycle has two **pedals**.
Pushing the pedals makes the wheels turn.

When we ride a bicycle, we push down on the pedals with our feet.

Push the Pedals

When we push the pedals, the wheels turn and the bicycle moves. The pedals **connect** to the back wheel with a bicycle chain.

bicycle chain

A bicycle chain goes around a part by the pedals. It also goes around a part on the back wheel. It makes the wheel turn when the pedals are pushed.

The bicycle chain helps the pedals make the wheels turn.

Something to Hold

How does the bicycle go where you want it to go? You use the **handlebars**!

handlebars

You turn the bike by turning the handlebars left or right. To go straight, you hold the handlebars still.

brakes

Many bikes have brakes on the handlebars. You squeeze the brakes to make the bicycle stop. Brakes are a technology that make riding a bicycle safer!

The Seat and Frame

A bicycle has a seat. It is a soft place for a rider to sit.

seat

You can move a bicycle seat up or down. This makes it just the right **height** for you!

A bicycle has a **frame**. It holds the parts together.

frame

This bicycle has a red frame. It connects the wheels, seat, pedals, and handlebars.

Every Part is Important

All of the parts of a bicycle work together. When all the parts work, the bicycle moves, turns, and stops. If one part is missing or broken, the bicycle will not work as it should.

If the bicycle chain is broken, the pedals cannot turn the wheels. Without handlebars, the bicycle cannot go where you want it to go. Without a seat, the bicycle is hard to ride. Every part is important.

Working Well

What other technologies have systems made of many parts?

helmet

scooter

A scooter is a technology. A helmet is a technology too. Both are made of parts. Can you think of the parts that help them work?

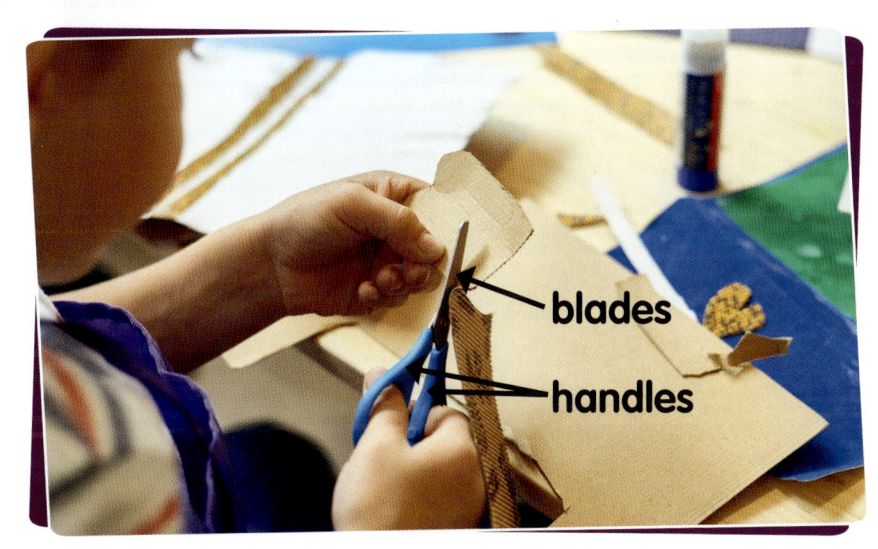

Scissors are a technology made of parts! They have handles to hold. They have two **blades** for cutting.

blades

handles

Do you like using computers? This technology is made of many big and small parts. The parts work together to help you learn, work, and play!

21

Words to Know

blades [bleyds] noun Flat parts of a tool that cut

connect [kuh-NEKT] verb To join together

frame [freym] noun A structure that joins or supports something

handlebars [HAN-duhl-bahrs] noun Part of a bicycle for hands to hold

height [hahyt] noun The highest part of something

lenses [lenz-es] noun Curved pieces of material, usually glass, that can be looked through

pedals [PEHD-ahls] noun Part of a bicycle for the feet to rest and push

protect [pruh-TEKT] verb To keep from being hurt

rays [reys] noun Beams of light coming from bright objects

system [sis-tuhm] noun A group of parts that form a whole

A noun is a person, place, or thing.
A verb is an action word that tells you what someone or something does.
An adjective is a word that tells you what something is like.

Index

bicycle parts 8–19
camera 7
computer 21
helmet 20
scissors 21

scooter 20
seesaw 5
sunglasses 6
working together 6–7, 8, 18–19

About the Author

Cynthia O'Brien has written many books for young readers. It is fun to help make a technology like a book! Books can be full of stories. They also teach you about the world around you, including other technologies.

To explore and learn more, enter the code at the Crabtree Plus website below.

www.crabtreeplus.com/fullsteamahead

Your code is:
fsa20

STEAM Notes for Educators

Full STEAM Ahead is a literacy series that helps readers build vocabulary, fluency, and comprehension while learning about big ideas in STEAM subjects. *Parts Work Together* helps readers identify main ideas in the text by establishing big ideas, repeating them, and using examples. The STEAM activity below helps readers extend the ideas in the book to build their skills in technology, arts, and science.

Systems and Predictions

Children will be able to:
- Understand how the parts of classroom or home technologies work together.
- Make predictions about what might happen if a part of a technology is missing.

Materials
- Made of Parts Worksheet
- Prediction Sheet
- Poster board and paper
- Materials for project, including boxes, paper, cardboard, glue, tape, craft sticks, paper rolls, and art materials

Guiding Prompts
After reading *Parts Work Together*, ask children:
- Can you name some examples of technologies that are made of many parts?
- Why is it important that all parts work as they should?

Activity Prompts
Have children explore the classroom or give them an evening to explore their homes. They should find a technology that is made of two or more parts. Have each child fill in the Made of Parts Worksheet in which they identify their technology and make a labeled diagram.

Have children pair up. They should switch their technologies and the accompanying Made of Parts Worksheet with their partner. Then, each child fills in the Prediction Sheet based on their partner's technology.

Have each child create a poster with the name of their technology, a good copy of their diagram, and the predictions that were made about their technology. Diagram should be in the center, with the rest of the poster as eye-catching as possible.

When posters are finished, hold a gallery walk in which children view each other's posters. Have a class discussion about the predictions, and the importance of parts that work together.

Extensions
- Find a simple, inexpensive technology with many parts. Have children make predictions about what might happen if various parts were missing. Then, remove one or more parts. See what happens and reflect on predictions.

To view and download the worksheets, visit **www.crabtreebooks.com/resources/printables** or **www.crabtreeplus.com/fullsteamahead** and enter the code **fsa20**.